Willy

Written by **Geert De Kockere** | Illustrated by **Carll Cneut**

Eerdmans Books for Young Readers

Grand Rapids, Michigan • Cambridge, U.K.

Willy had legs like pillars.

Four of them.

And a body as big as two.

But only one, thank goodness.

He had two huge ears that flapped in the wind.

And in between was his head,

with a trunk that dangled from it.

He also had a tail

(an insignificant little thing)

with a ridiculous little brush at the end.

And still . . .

And still Willy was invited everywhere.

To come and stand —

that he could do extremely well.

Even on one leg.

He never lost his balance.

He stood like a mast.

That came in very handy

when you needed someone to hold something —

a clothesline full of laundry, for instance.

He was also often invited

to come and listen.

He could do that very well, too —

with those two big ears of his.

He heard everything.

He heard the pros and he heard the cons;

he heard the sobs and he heard the sighs.

He was also invited everywhere to paint.

Especially the really fine details.

Willy was very good at that —

with that little brush at the end of his tail.

Nobody could do it like he could.

He could draw the finest lines.

And he always dotted the i's.

Willy was even asked to join the choir.

To keep the beat with his trunk.

He did that very well.

Six-eight time or three-four time —

he didn't mind.

Willy beat them all.

Sometimes he was called on to come and push

with that enormous body of his.

A child who didn't want to go to school,

or a car that stood in the way.

Willy pushed them along,

just like that.

Like a feather.

Willy was also in demand to come and sit.

In the front row.

During a play at the theater, for instance.

Because Willy always sat very properly —

on that big behind of his.

Straight as an arrow. Without wiggling.

It didn't take any effort.

Not even when the play was boring,

and he fell asleep.

Willy never leaned over.

Never.

And thus Willy went from here to there,

from small griefs to big quarrels.

To listen to one side and then to the other.

He visited art and writing groups.

To paint.

And to dot the i's.

He marched with brass bands and parades.

To keep the beat. Usually two-four.

He went to the opera and the theater,

sitting still until late at night.

One time

he also participated in the elections.

To push the candidates.

With that enormous body of his.

It was a piece of cake.

So Willy was seldom at home.

And he was welcome everywhere.

Very welcome. Extremely welcome.

Now and then someone made a remark.

About the legs like pillars. Or about his enormous ears.

Or about that little tail on his big behind.

But those remarks were brushed off very quickly.

Or overruled. Even swept away.

Then, Willy was comforted.

With many arms. And much warmth.

So if you have legs like pillars

or ears that flap in the wind,

or if you have a body as big as two,

or arms that dangle;

if you have a little something somewhere,

with a ridiculous little brush at the end,

then think of him.

Think of Willy.

HE HAD IT ALL.

Geert De Kockere is a Belgian author who has written numerous books for children. His work has been translated into at least eight languages. He is also an avid nature photographer, and has published four books of his photographs. Visit his website at www.geertdekockere.be.

Carll Cneut has illustrated over thirty books, including *The Amazing Love Story of Mister Morf* (Macmillan) as well as *City Lullaby* and *Ten Moonstruck Piglets* (both Clarion). He has won many awards for his work, including the Book Peacock award for the Belgian edition of *Willy*. In 2010 he was shortlisted for the Hans Christian Andersen Award. Carll lives in Belgium. Visit his website at www.carllcneut.com.

Original Title: *Willy*
© 1999 by Uitgeverij De Eenhoorn, Vlasstraat 17, B-8710 Wielsbeke, Belgium
Text by Geert De Kockere
Illustrations by Carll Cneut

This edition published in 2011 by
Eerdmans Books for Young Readers,
an imprint of
Wm. B. Eerdmans Publishing Co.
2140 Oak Industrial Dr. NE, Grand Rapids, Michigan 49505
P.O. Box 163, Cambridge CB3 9PU U.K.

www.eerdmans.com/youngreaders

Manufactured at Tien Wah Press, in Singapore, March 2011, first edition

11 12 13 14 15 16 17   8 7 6 5 4 3 2 1

Library of Congress Cataloging-in-Publication Data
Kockere, Geert De, 1962-
[Willy. English]
Willy / by Geert De Kockere; illustrated by Carll Cneut.
p. cm.
Summary: Willy the elephant has everything an elephant should have,
from four sturdy legs to a tail with a little brush on the end.
ISBN 978-0-8028-5395-0 (alk. paper)
[1. Elephants — Fiction.] I. Cneut, Carll, ill. II. Title.
PZ7.K81744Wi 2011
[E] — dc22
2010049545